The Backyard

The Backyard

JOHN COLLIER

VIKING

VIKING

Published by the Penguin Group

Penguin Books USA Inc., 375 Hudson Street, New York, New York 10014, U.S.A.

Penguin Books Ltd, 27 Wrights Lane, London W8 5TZ, England

Penguin Books Australia Ltd, Ringwood, Victoria, Australia

Penguin Books Canada Ltd, 10 Alcorn Avenue, Toronto, Ontario, Canada M4V 3B2

Penguin Books (N.Z.) Ltd, 182–190 Wairau Road, Auckland 10, New Zealand

Penguin Books Ltd, Registered Offices: Harmondsworth, Middlesex, England

First published in 1993 by Viking, a division of Penguin Books USA Inc.

10 9 8 7 6 5 4 3 2 1

Copyright © John Collier, 1993   All rights reserved

Library of Congress Cataloging-in-Publication Data

Collier, John. The backyard/written and illustrated by John Collier.   p.   cm.

Summary: A child imagines what has taken place in the backyard,

from the present all the way back to the creation of the world.

ISBN 0-670-83609-5

[1. History—Fiction.] I. Title.

PZ7.C679Ba 1993[E]—dc20   93-14661 CIP AC

Printed in Singapore   Set in 22 point Goudy Old Style

To my father,
who taught me to love art,
and my mother,
who taught me to love libraries

In my backyard
is a wide lawn,
where birds sing,
and dogs run,

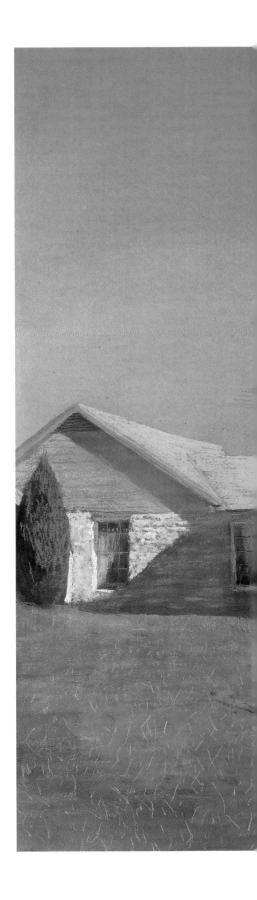

and my mother plants it
and my father cuts it,
all in my backyard.

But before that,
carpenters came,
who staked the ground
and raised the wood,

and hammered the boards,
and sweated and laughed,
from dawn to dusk,
and sang songs I never heard,
all in my backyard.

And before that,
came plows and horses
and farm boys and cows,

and cowboys
sang lonesome songs
and died on cold plains
—all in my backyard.

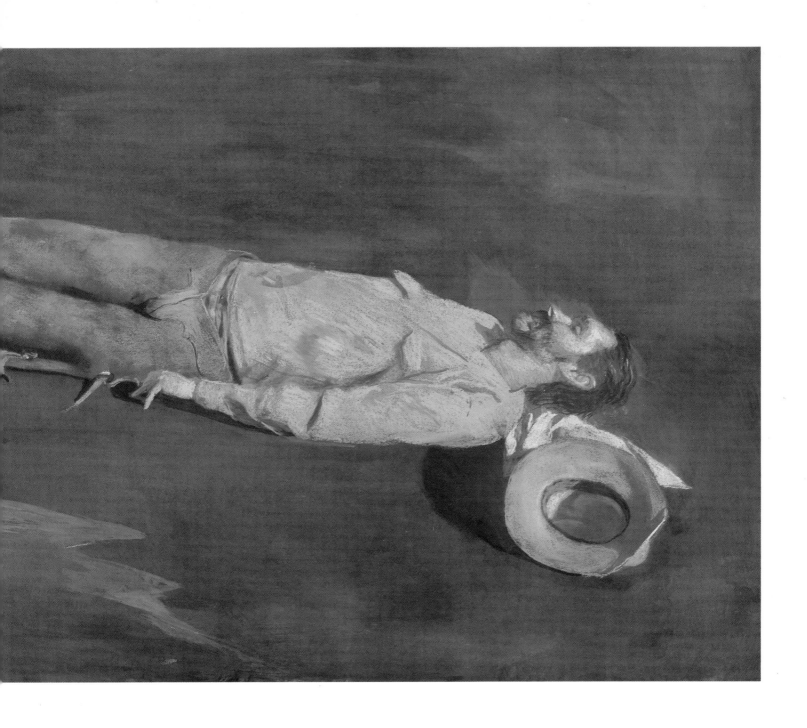

Braves loved maidens,
and great battles with no names raged

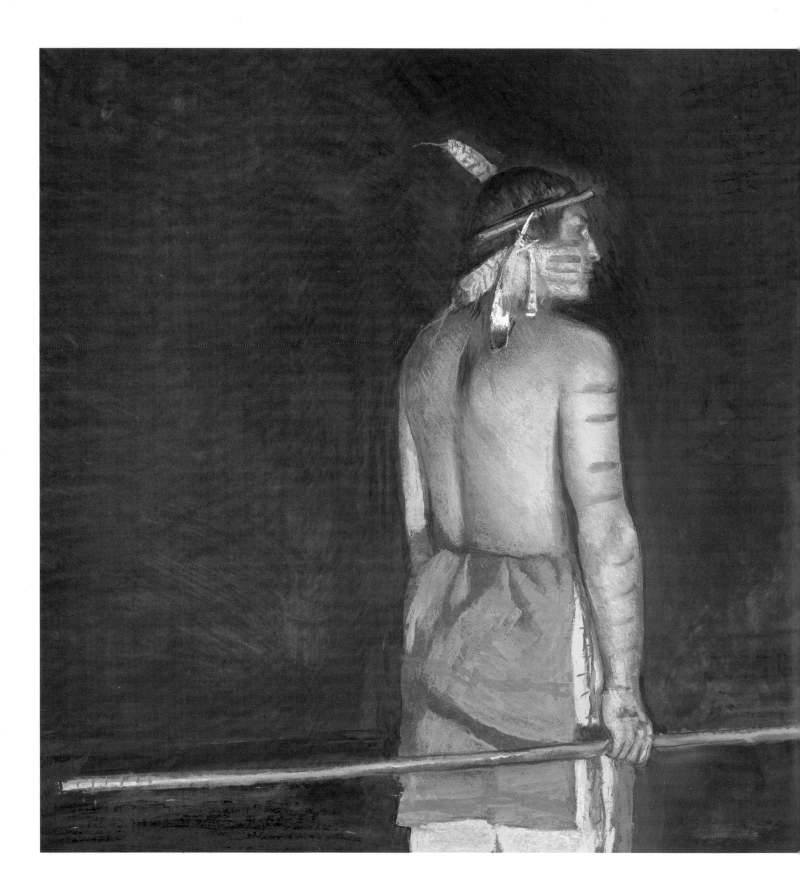

and chiefs walked like giants
and breathed air
that no man had ever breathed
—all in my backyard.

And great mammoths
waved their trunks
and dinosaurs walked
the shores of seas
no sailor ever saw

and fishes swam
and mountains rose
and mountains fell
—all in my backyard.

Volcanoes rose out of lifeless seas
that beat them to gravel
and fires hot as a hundred forges

and hydrogen and darkness
and the hand of God moved

all in my backyard.